Shy Little Kitten's
Secret Place

By Jim Lawrence
Illustrated by Keenan Jones

A GOLDEN BOOK • NEW YORK
Western Publishing Company, Inc., Racine, Wisconsin 53404

There is a magical place called Little Golden Book Land, filled with wonderful things to see and do. Every day is a special day, just waiting to be discovered.

It was a warm summer day in Little Golden Book Land, and a group of roly-poly kittens was romping around outside.

"Let's play hide-and-seek!" said one.

"Oh, yes, yes! Let's!" said another.

What fun it was, hiding in the grass or under a bush, trying not to be seen by whoever was it! And what shouting and shrieking there was when someone was discovered.

"Here *I* am," said a small, timid voice. Shy Little Kitten peeked out from behind a tree, smiling hopefully.

But no one paid any attention. "They don't even miss me," she thought sadly.

Just then Tootle rode by. "Who wants to ride out to the lighthouse?" he called.

"I do! I do!" shouted the kittens all at once.

"Then hop on!" said the puppies from next door, who had already boarded the train. They were all there except Poky Little Puppy. He was still running along behind Katy Caboose, his ears flapping wildly as he tried to catch up.

He was finally able to climb aboard when Tootle stopped for the kittens. But one of them got left behind as the train started to chug again.

"Please! Wait for me," cried Shy Little Kitten, jumping out of her hiding place. "I want to come, too!"

But no one could hear her timid little voice over all the fuss and excitement.

She chased the train down toward Main Street as fast as her little legs would carry her. But by the time she got there, Tootle and Katy Caboose were almost out of sight.

Scuffy the tugboat was sailing across the harbor.
Shy little kitten waved one tiny paw and called to
him. "Can you see the train?" she asked. She hoped
he might somehow help her catch up with it.

But Scuffy didn't answer. He didn't notice the small,
bashful bundle of fur trying to get his attention.

By now the trainload of merrymakers had
completely disappeared around the curving shoreline
that wound its way out to Lighthouse Point.

Shy Little Kitten felt so lonely.

She trudged up the mountain, farther than she had ever gone alone. She saw Saggy Baggy Elephant galumphing around on his hind legs, squirting coconut juice at his pal Tawny Scrawny Lion.

She wished she could join in the fun…but she didn't want to get in the way.

Still farther up the mountain Baby Brown Bear was bouncing a ball back and forth with his father, Big Brown Bear. Every so often they would stop to scoop honey from a nearby hollow tree.

Shy Little Kitten gave a timid cough. "Could I play, too?" she asked. "I could roll the ball with my nose, and I…er…love honey."

Baby Brown Bear saw her and waved a sticky paw. But Shy Little Kitten could tell he hadn't really heard her. He was too busy having fun.

"It's my own fault," she said wistfully. "If only I were bold enough to speak up and make people pay more attention. I bet I'd have lots more fun."

Shy Little Kitten wandered on. It wasn't fun exploring all by herself. But she hadn't anything better to do.

Suddenly she saw a big opening in a nearby slope. "Looks like a cave," she thought. "I wonder who lives there."

She peered in timidly. "Anybody home?" she called.

Nobody was, but her own voice boomed back, louder than she had ever heard it before: "ANYBODY HOME?! ANYBODY HOME?!"

Shy Little Kitten grinned happily. She decided to venture farther in. She saw the most wonderful bumpy walls, and rocks of all shapes and sizes.

With one small paw she slowly pushed a pebble. Then she pushed it again and again. Before she knew it, Shy Little Kitten was having the time of her life.

"Now, this is fun! THIS IS FUN!" she shouted, and her now-bold voice echoed throughout the cave.

"I'm not shy in here," she thought, "and I like it!"

One day Shy Little Kitten was in her secret cave, jumping from boulder to boulder, when she remembered that the Little Golden Book Land Egg Hunt was taking place that day.

She did a quick somersault and a triple flip-flop to the ground and was about to join the others in the hunt. But she was having such a good time, she decided to stay and play a while longer.

In the meantime, everyone else had already begun their search for eggs.

Poky Little Puppy was lagging behind as usual. He kept looking all around and sniffling here and there for eggs.

"Where's Shy Little Kitten?" he wondered out loud.

The only answers he got were shrugs. No one had seen her all morning, and no one seemed to be having much luck finding eggs, either.

"Hey! There's a good place to look," Saggy Baggy Elephant hollered hopefully. "A cave!"

Strange sounds could be heard as they got closer to the cave. Startled, the group stopped and clasped hands before continuing on. They slowly walked inside, but they stopped suddenly!

They saw Shy Little Kitten — or at least someone who looked like Shy Little Kitten — but she clearly wasn't acting shy anymore!

"Hi, gang!" she yowled, in between all the other
noises she was making. Shy Little Kitten was
screeching and meowing and caterwauling at the top
of her tiny lungs.

And Shy Little Kitten wasn't only making a lot of
noise. She was climbing the bumpy walls, then
running around the cave like crazy — jumping here
and there and everywhere! Then she was batting
pebbles across the floor of the cave like a hockey
player on ice!

"Well? What are you all staring at?" asked Shy Little
Kitten when she had worn herself out for the moment.

"At you!" they all gasped.

"What's gotten into you?" asked Poky Little Puppy.

"Nothing's gotten *into* me," she said gaily. "It's just
the real me coming *out*! It took a lot of practice in my
secret cave. First I had to get used to my voice being
very loud. The echo in here really helped. Now I just
love to YELL and YELL at the top of my lungs.

"Then I started to explore. At first I only climbed the little ledges, but soon I made my way to the top of all the big boulders and could even hang upside down. Now I know how to have fun like everyone else!

"Speaking of fun," Shy Little Kitten added, "isn't the egg hunt still going on?"

When everyone nodded, still not quite over the change in their little friend, Shy Little Kitten said, "Well, then, let's go, gang!"

Bursting out of the cave, she led the other egg hunters all over the mountain.

And guess who found the most eggs?